# Sleeping Cinderella

## and Other Princess Mix-ups

STORY BY **STEPHANIE CLARKSON**

PICTURES BY **BRIGETTE BARRAGER**

**ORCHARD BOOKS • NEW YORK**

An Imprint of Scholastic Inc.

For Romy and Olivia, who are so over princesses.

For Merryn, who much prefers dinosaurs.

And for Dan, who loved this. — S.C.

Text copyright © 2015 by Stephanie Clarkson
Illustrations copyright © 2015 by Brigette Barrager

Library of Congress Cataloging-in-Publication Data
Clarkson, Stephanie.
Sleeping Cinderella and other princess mix-ups / by Stephanie Clarkson ;
illustrated by Brigette Barrager.   pages   cm
Summary: Cinderella, Snow White, Sleeping Beauty, and Rapunzel are all unhappy, but when they decide to switch places for a day each discovers what she likes—and what she can change—about her own life.
ISBN 978-0-545-56564-6 (hardcover)—ISBN 978-0-545-56744-2 (e-book)  [1. Stories in rhyme. 2. Princesses—Fiction. 3. Contentment—Fiction. 4. Humorous stories.] I. Barrager, Brigette, illustrator. II. Title.
PZ8.3.C54855Sle 2015    E]—dc23       2014014464
10 9 8 7 6 5 4 3 2 1                    15 16 17 18 19
Printed in Malaysia       108
First printing, February 2015

The display type was set in Shelley Volante Script. The text was set in Charlotte Book.
The illustrations were created digitally. Book design by Chelsea C. Donaldson

nce upon a time . . .

four fairy tale misses,
tired of dwarves, witches, princes, and kisses,
so bored and fed up, or just ready to flop,
upped and left home for a fairy tale swap. . . .

"Enough!" cried Snow White, and she threw down her broom.

She stared in disgust at the state of the room.

The sink was piled high with cups and with plates.

Snow White moaned, "I'm so tired of these sloppy housemates!"

So Snow White walked out,
left her dwarf friends behind,
hoping that someplace
less messy she'd find.
She walked and she walked,
for hour upon hour,
until, in the distance,
she spotted a tower.

In a window up high, there appeared a pale face.
"Hi!" Snow White yelled. "Is this really your place?"
Rapunzel called, "Yes, but I wish it was not.

It's lonely up here. I miss people a lot."

home
sweet
tower

"One room with a view,"
Snow White cried. "Oh, what bliss!

I can't think of any home nicer than this!"

"You move in, I'll move out," said the girl with long hair.

"You'll be all by yourself—

you won't have to share!"

So *Rapunzel* left *Snow* and the tower behind,

hoping that someplace more lively she'd find.

She walked and she walked till she noticed a teen

in glass slippers and gown, royal as a queen.

"Hey," said Rapunzel. "You off somewhere fun?
I'm loving those shoes and that coach built for one."
"My godmother's sending me off to a ball,"
yawned the girl, "but I just can't be bothered at all."

"I've been slaving for weeks—my name's *Cinderella*.

I want a night's sleep, not to dance with some fella."

"I see," said *Rapunzel*. "There's no need to stress!

I'll go in your place if you just change your dress."

So *Cinderella* left *Rapunzel* behind,

hoping that someplace more restful she'd find.

She walked and she walked till thorns ripped her coat.

Then all of a sudden, she spotted a moat.

In the castle,

a maiden with crown on her head,

slept on the comfiest, springiest bed.

*Cinderella* leaned over,

but—whoops!—down she fell!

Her lips brushed the girl, who awoke with a yell.

"Sorry," cried *Cinderella*. "What poor form!
But I badly need sleep, and your bed looks so warm."
"No worries," said *Beauty*. "I've no time to lose!
I'm 'Sleeping' no longer, so please take a snooze."

Yes, *Beauty* was glad to leave the girl reclined,

hoping that someplace more thrilling she'd find.

She walked till a house in a clearing she spied,

with two smoking chimneys and a door open wide.

Creeping inside, *Beauty* felt her heart flutter.

She saw several dwarves trapped beneath piles of clutter!

"Gracious," said *Beauty*. "Shall I help with that?

I long to be busy, to work, and to chat."

But sooner, not later, real problems took place.

*Beauty* cried, "Someone keeps shoving food in my face!

I'm not keen on apples from people in hoods.

But a grandma keeps trying to give me her goods!"

Back home, *Beauty* found *Cinderella* dismayed.

"Your prince friend just kissed me awake, I'm afraid.

I'm sorry to say, but he's rather a flirt.

Plus, this spinning wheel's sharp.

Someone's gonna get hurt!"

Cinderella ran home, up hill and down slope,
and found Rapunzel at the end of her rope.
"I've lost a glass shoe and your sisters are rude.
I was riding in style till your coach turned to food!"

Then, in pain, *Rapunzel* limped off to her tower,

to soak her tired feet and to take a hot shower.

*Snow White* was still there, but as bored as could be.

She said, "Phew! Am I glad that you're home finally!

"I'm missing my dwarves,
I'm forlorn and bereft.
Plus, you didn't mention
a witch when you left!
She's possessive and clingy,
too needy, I find.
I can't wait to leave here.
I hope you don't mind."

So back home at last, each girl called a meeting.

*Snow* sat her dwarves down on their miniature seating.

She said, "Cleaning for seven is leaving me sore.

We'll get along fine if we each have a chore."

TO-DO
LIST:
• sweep
• vacuum
• dishes
• mop
• scrub
• polish
• laundry
• windows
• water
  plants

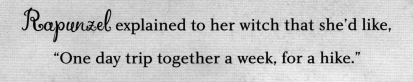

Rapunzel explained to her witch that she'd like,
"One day trip together a week, for a hike."

Cinderella went off to college instead,
met a regular guy—less well-off but well-read.

"I'm so over spinning," poor *Beauty* decreed.

"From now on I'll knit stuff, and then I won't bleed."

So, by talking things through and her problems amending,

each girl truly made her own *fairy tale* ending.